This is Not a Stunt

Cath Nichols

Valley Press

First published in 2017 by Valley Press
Woodend, The Crescent, Scarborough, YO11 2PW
www.valleypressuk.com

First edition, first printing (August 2017)

ISBN 978-1-908853-86-8
Cat. no. VP0103

A CIP record for this book is available from the British Library.

Cover and text design by Jamie McGarry.
Edited by Martha Sprackland.

Printed and bound in Great Britain by
Imprint Digital, Upton Pyne, Exeter.

THIS IS NOT A STUNT

Cath Nichols was born in Kent, 1970, but spent her childhood in Papua New Guinea and New Zealand. She is the author of two pamphlets, *Tales of Boy Nancy* (Driftwood, 2005) and *Distance* (Erbacce Press, 2012) and a collection, *My Glamorous Assistant* (Headland, 2007). She holds a PhD in Creative Writing.

Dedication

To the rockers and rollers, the stout and the frail,
the shakers and twitchers, the sprats and the whales,
the droolers and smilers, the cis and the trans,
the seers and signers, those with/without hands,
to the limpers and gimpers, the fast and the slow,
the noisy and flappy, the chatty, the still,
those raving, those hoping, the mad, the insane,
the ones who are doubting, the ones who can sing.

To those who are spectrum'd, each one of us jewels,
to the steady, the flagging, the wise and us fools.
The queer and the unqueer, the short and the tall,
the paid-up, the paid-down, the not-paid-at-all.
The dark-skinned, the light-skinned, the crooked, the straight,
the freaks and the weirdos, our families, our mates.
To the activist gliding or marching along, and
each witness, each pray-er, who can't leave their home.

To the readers, the feelers, those with/without rules,
to everyone living and all yet to come.
To those doing, those done to, the done for, the done,
those choosing, the chosen – those who are gone.
To all of us still being caught in our dreams,
to the thinkers: the thought of us – making a scene!

Acknowledgments

'Steel' won second prize in the 2008 Poetry on the Lake competition and appeared in that year's journal (volume 1). 'Woman Standing' was a finalist in the 2009 Aesthetica poetry competition and was published in that year's anthology. 'Toni & Guy' appeared in *Sculpted: Poetry of the North West* (eds. Lindsay Holland & Angela Topping, 2013). Three poems have appeared in *Stairs and Whispers: D/deaf and Disabled Poets Write Back* (Nine Arches Press, 2017).

Other poems have appeared in *Cake* (Lancaster University), *The Literary Nest, Lumen* (Edinburgh University), *Poetry Salzburg, Poetry Wales, The Stinging Fly, Storm Cellar, Under the Radar* and The Lonely Page 2011 conference proceedings (Queen's University Belfast, e-sharp publications).

Some of the *Bo(d)y-in-waiting* poems were discussed by myself in 'Intersections Between Disability and Trans*: A Poetics', a chapter in *Reflections on Female and Trans* Masculinities* (Cambridge Scholars Publishing, 2016). Thanks to Jude and Nina for organising the conference that led to the book. Some of this sequence was also presented and discussed at research seminars at Liverpool Hope University and Edge Hill University. Thanks to Dr David Bolt, Claire Penketh and to Lisa Davies.

Thanks to Jamie McGarry at Valley Press and Martha Sprackland. Special thanks to my family and partner, and to Dr Mari Hughes-Edwards who kept on at me to get these poems to a publisher.

Contents

Sleep Experiment

I dream of a baby too small to be cradled,
head lolling on its stalk, no good
in my pocket or palm. The baby dies.
I will go into the garden now.

The sleep scientist says I shouldn't fret
so much. REM sleep is not the only sleep
with dreams. We dream turn by turn in waves
that phase throughout the night.

I dream of a house and a cat walks in,
skeletal, and folds herself into
the fire's surround. 'She has cancer,'
someone says. 'It's not because we starve her.'

One tide positive, the next negative. Nightmares
have a function, he says. Trouble lets us
practice fight or flight whilst sleeping.
We spark fresh neural pathways.

The cat's body shrinks till just
her creased-skull head remains, intricate
as a scarab. Next there is a garden,
walled and dank, a blackened square,

it happens every night not just the nights
we fell afraid and woke exhausted. The scientist
says we recall the dreams we do
because we are disturbed and briefly wake;

such surfacing prints a memory for morning.
But if we were to wake in another
sleep cycle we might recall cats purring,
babies flying, the garden singing.

Dreams are our vestigial legs, our sealed-up gills,
the bumps beneath our still-evolving skin.
I will wake soon and go. I will go into the garden,
plant seeds. I will wake and go. It really is my garden.

Accommodation

They would like to be executives
in smart suits and ties but their faces
don't quite fit the corporate divine,

with their cleft noses, hooks for hands,
fur where others' skin is smooth. The room
booked for interview failed to provide

adaptations. Roosts. Bat applicants tried
to stand but dizziness ensued, then bumps
and bruises. I wish the senior manager

had seen those bats last night, wheeling, fast
and light across the evening sky, catching moths
and gnats on the curve, returning to roost

in the smallest of spaces, adept and economical.
Bats are glorious and smart but will never
make the grade if we insist on polyester,

keep regulation offices where workers
stare askance at
fur, flight and leather wings.

Dull

In bed, there is a sound of running water, maybe drains
or something in the gutter, I don't know which,
there's something wrong with my ears.

Perhaps the sound is from the bathroom, a tap
left on? My partner gestures to the window '… kale?'
But I didn't hear the gale last night

despite this constant whishing. I can't detect
the central heating's tick, the gurgles from
our frost-free fridge, all background sound is gone –

it's something to do with pitch. I don't hear
my partner in the shower, the kettle boiling,
the car leaving. I worry

about taps left on. I miss birdsong.

Everyone is King Canute

Busy getting on with our lives, we move
away from what seems vast, from difference,

so busy, busy forgetting
slippage, vulnerabilities,

we frown, tell the tide to turn away,
fail to make our lives solid,

cannot bear this knowledge.
Each body is an act of becoming,

not permanent, not magic. We go on
in our habits, refuse the evidence,

refuse to see we're fiction.

Cloth Ears

The suicidal fall of tiny hairs
housed in the inner ear: traumatic or
age-related hearing loss. In a book
by David Lodge, the narrator,
a Professor of Linguistics, starts to lose
his hearing, so retires. Students, we read,
can only concentrate on speech
for twenty minutes at a time,
unless that speech is broken up
with recap, discussion, Q&A.
Susurration makes speech a struggle.
Turning up one's hearing aid produces
such a squeal of noise it tries the nerves.
There are looks, sniggers, non-sequiturs.
Without hearing our hero cannot engage
in hard-surfaced lecture halls.
Blindness in literature asserts itself
as tragic, deafness as comic, claims Lodge.
Consider church beer. Sorry,
Shakespeare. (Lip-reading is difficult too.)
The blind are seers and oracles. The deaf
are dumb, or won't try hard enough.
Even amongst the liberal classes, impatience
is rife: 'Have You Got It In?' 'HAVE YOU
CHECKED THE BATTERIES?' (Excuse my whine,
plastic is not perfect.) To return to the book:
one Christmas night our hero's wife
tells Lena, 'Grandpa's an Eeyore'.
Later the Prof rifles through
his childhood copy of Winnie-the-Pooh,
tracking the grey beast down.

There's the donkey on his birthday, raising
a hoof to press his ear forwards,
wobbling on his three remaining legs.
'Look at Eeyore!' we laugh at the picture.
'Look! Poor Eeyore's deaf!'

Heard

Nothing as bright as a blackbird's eye
rimmed gold and that sideways

look. Nothing as odd
as phhtt phhtt, phhtt phhtt

wings washed in rain flicking
a primrose styrofoam tray.

Wash your hands
before you leave toilet

I have seen some individuals leaving the toilet without washing thier hands, these people are rather extremely arogant and dirty as they leave their genital germs on everything that they touch, those germs are ingested/swallowed by others as they use or touch the same things that these dirty people have touched without washing their hands.

Circled in thin red pen: 'thier' and 'arogant'.
Red observes a 'run on sentence', judges
'6/10 see me.' A further comment in thick black ink:
'Nice to see OCD is still prevalent amongst the academic classes.'

We live too close and side by side.

thier   arogant

Keeping Score

Fingers shut like dominoes
falling away from touch.
We talk, but cannot
get the thing to fit.
The door is not kept locked
yet we both stay. We cannot
shape this dance
any better than we
can shape our children.

Should I stay?

I used to think it a sign of weakness:
uncertainty, doubt, but now I'm not so sure.
Leaving lovers, towns, religions, I was fearless –
used to think it a sign of weakness
to stay and wait things out, hope for the best.
These days, babies spring to mind, bathwater.
I used to think it a sign of weakness,
uncertainty, doubt, but now I'm not so sure.

I am extremely sorry for the delay and for any inconvenience this may cause to your journey.

I'm sorry I didn't get there on time, my train was delayed
due to stopping at additional stations.
I'm sorry I couldn't get you a message. My train was delayed
due to a fire in the Penrith area.
I'm sorry I didn't text or call. You see, my train
with its leaves on the line… There's always an excuse.
Leaves crushed on rails are dangerous,
slippery, becoming hard.
I'm sorry I didn't tell you before you found out
for yourself. That last announcement said
this train has been delayed due to animals on the track,
my heart went out to them, still, I wanted to move on.
Later there was more detail: cows on the line
in the Hartford area. I thought of your wet dark eyes.

Vocation

My mother used to play cricket for the county
under-sixteens, but me? Never had that moment

as a champion gymnast teen.
At twenty-two, I could have been a skater

in Seoul (I lie, my chance was
only ever in Barcelona.)

A swimmer, then? Hard pressed for Sydney
at thirty, and not with these ears.

Later, I consider ballroom, a dance
that might move me – the waltz, the quickstep,

the American Smooth. Go easy on the lifts
and make my partner extra sturdy.

Athens, Beijing pass me by. Rowing
in London, perhaps? But think of my knees.

Brazil. Is there time to train my eye
on cues and pockets, to snooker balls across

green baize? Is there time to conjugate
the arrows and concentric rings of darts?

Tokyo. I would so like a clear sightline,
a running flight-line, to soar before the game is over,

I always liked to tell a story with my hands.

Travel, age 6 (found text)

I am playing with my toy
train railway line. It is
red. The carpet is blue.

I can telephone my
friends. I telephone my
sister's friend when she
wants me too. It is fun

to telephone friends. It is
fun to play with friends.
It is fun.

In six days' time it will be
my sister's birthday. She
has four children to come
to her birthday. If she

had seven children she
would have to sell the
presents.

My friend is sleeping
on a campbed. He is
sleeping in my
bedroom. It is a

little bedroom. I like
Him sometimes.
Dad has got a job.

He has got the job in
England. Sometime in
June we are going to
England. Mum said

we could go to England very
soon. We are going to have
one night on the plane.

On Sunday I made
some people. I made
a pony. I made a tree.
I put all of them in a box.

Then I put the box away
in the cardboard.

Arc, age 16

Our steady pace across the field transformed each sapling
into an upturned basket; the farmer called it 'tying down
the apple trees'. It was our first job that summer and we were eager
to try others. We soon learnt it was the best job. The others:
picking runner beans (piecework, we never made much money),
picking strawberries (fat berries turned sea anemone, a flailing
mass of maggots in our hands), and we worked the packing sheds
(mangetout, mainly). By the conveyor belt, a lot of talk.

This was our life with older women, our south-east Wild West.
Me and my sister coveted The Body, a man with muscled chest,
riding tanned on his tractor. He stapled his thumb
to a crate one day, but mostly he glowed in the distance.
We were asked to the pub, but never went. Scared, I guess.
We didn't fit with the locals, weren't ready yet to pass.

Toni & Guy

THE UNION

The gay scene exists in the red light district, in a few minging basement bars let out on weekday nights. It is 1978, Manchester. You are eighteen and a man asks you to be a hair model. He likes your sharp male features. Vidal Sassoon is something new, the hub of something hot. Gay men fancy you, straight women fancy you and lesbians do too. You play bass in a band, support Joy Division, you are The Distractions.

PARADISE

Your band gets signed to Factory Records up on Paradise Street. You're later signed to Island. The old office becomes a club, the Paradise Factory. I meet friends at Manto's then queue for Paradise. Manto's is Canal Street's first gay bar with floor-to-ceiling windows, a revolution in visibility. We display our Flesh at the Hacienda, drink water. Wave our hands in the air. We do, we do care.

POPTASTIC 96

'We're here, we're queer, and we're not going shopping!' Except of course we are, overcome with amazement that we carry a pink pound. A glossy mag for gay gals has arrived: *Diva,* a national monthly. With its personal ads and pictures, we're so excited pre-web. When we tire of Paradise, its techno-beats and dykes in Wonderbras, we go to Poptastic, dance to indie-pop in grungy boots. We marvel at the underage: the baby-dyke.

VELVET

When I am twenty-eight a man in Poptastic touches my hair. So he touches me. No one touches a No.1 without stroking the fuzzy pelt of it. And this is post-rave, post-E, when we all drink beer, so the guy that fondles my head is a little too forward, a little too straight. But he is a straight hairdresser – who wants to *hand cut* my skinhead. He gives me his number. He works at Toni & Guy.

CRUZ 101

I wonder if a cut will feel different to a shave? I go to the salon, let him snip-snip away, but it feels the same. Someone bleaches my hair. I look ill. Without the example of David Beckham – his thousand-quid blond skinhead – I don't think this cut could've happened. I walk the catwalk with a riding crop. David makes me a hair model; you and I cruise parallel lives.

SPIRIT 2000

Do you remember Anna we all had a crush on? The year *Big Brother* was new and exciting, the year you and I started dating. Anna was kind and funny, had been a nun. She played guitar and sang, and had a girlfriend. Maybe she'd cropped her hair when she was a novice, but it's chin-length on TV. She is more than the sum of her parts. It's the year I let my hair grow out, the year I grow it long.

The Other Stuff

She said she had to write it down. Her grandmother
kept telling the story over and over. She said this

with a 'tch' and a roll of her eyes. I said
you know, I think it's OK to say the same thing

over and over. In fact, my Dad might be going
that way, in fact sometimes even I

don't remember the stories I've told. Hers
was the story of how her gran and granddad met.

My friend is young and full of desire to see
and hear, taste and smell, newness, over and over.

But when you get older what matters
is being around the people you love, and writing

it down won't stop us from telling things
over and over. She smiled, *Yeah, you can talk*

about Big Brother with your friends at any time,
but the other stuff – you can only talk about that with them.

Hir m'Aphrodite

Blossom morning blue said the dark song

teach these wild tongues
to lace secrets

   sister not skin

Leaves crack the avenue,
dirt-bruised sound

       love in spite of

Each glassy evening burns

       love because of

         We stagger away,

       love along with

run tendrils through hir hair.

Migration of the Brown-Grey Unicorn

Leptonycteris yerbabuenae

Cumular volcanic ash, we rise
as shoals of fish, strength in numbers,

mesmerise our predators then
travel north to mate.

Each night we feed on nectar, pollinate
tequila flowers. Our bellies swell

with babies. Further north
we dunk our tipsy bodies

into goblet flowers of cacti.
The birthing cave is almost underground

and in its farthest caverns we hang
hairless jelly babies upside-down,

pink sugar mice that oscillate.
Each newborn pup's umbilical

strikes a brown vertical,
shivering withered grasses

that vibrate with tender noise.

The Return

His fur shows small bubbles
in the water. Silvery spots,
minute ball-bearing flecks. Michael
kept this clipping from the local paper.

He's written in the margin: *Four-legged yet*
water-gifted, to outfish fish, Ted Hughes.
I read the article, stare at the photograph.
Torrent is an otter cub afraid of the water.

He was rescued from the recent flood.
His hairs should lie sleek like
a seal's waxy pelt, but instead
his pimpled skin gasps for breath.

II. WOMAN STANDING

This woman on TV last night
said her daughter killed herself
at eighteen. She trims flowers
for her grave. *You have to accept it,*
she says. *You have to wait.*

My son has no grave except the ocean;
flowers are of no use. So, today?
Today I pull out the drawer
where my towel and swimsuit
lie curled. I stand and wait.

III. STEEL

Once I was neat and useful, sharp,
round-headed as a pin. Now

I am blank, headless. Your death
has split something.

What is this hole in my side?
The sea wind blows through me.

I have become a needle,
without cloth, without thread.

IV. WAVELENGTH

Sky is changed by the presence of birds,
white threads come loose from other cloth.

This sky is frayed, woven over
with the black clamour of birds. A cry

vibrates from throats and bones and wings,
bass clef, white noise. I hear static

sound turning.
Behind, the clouds hum.

Reading Would Save Me

I thought something would change, but it didn't.
I thought reading would save me. It hasn't.
I expected to grow up. I have grown inward.
There are circles and chasing and somebody's tail.

I thought reading would save me. It hasn't –
someone marked out a finish line.
There are circles and chasing and somebody's tail.
Not a rat's. Not a rat's race, no.

Someone marked out a finish line,
imported a wheel, metal rungs, spokes.
Not a rat's. Not a rat's race, no.
I'd give anything for a friendly face. Who

imported a wheel, metal rungs, spokes?
I thought something would change but it didn't.
I'd give anything for a friendly face. Who
expected to grow up?

Blink

The fluffy chick is not a fluffy chick,
it is hard-wired tendon and bone
made to gape and put on weight,
wear its parents down, a machine

with no memory, just instinct.
The Black Box is not a black box,
it is an orange-pink, a colour
to be found in wreckage,

it is an approximate sphere
to resist fracture on impact,
a rune, a recorder
to play back upon death.

The heart is not heart-shaped,
nor pink. It is a grey-maroon,
the colour of late mourning,
or a dull anatomy class. It is

a pulsing lump, knuckled with
pipes and orifices, made to pump
haemoglobin, a push-me pull-you animal,
made to maintain a constant pressure.

It is a flight recorder, a rune to be read,
as unlike your first love as it's possible to be.
It is red-grey, red-grey, red.

The Violence of

the poet enjoys sensation. She jabs out the title
'Outside the Operating Room of the Sex Change Doctor',
makes a row of penises the aftermath of something.

What is there might have mushroomed out of torture, war
or concentration camps. She gives voice to the penises,
stokes a ghoulish horror. But male-to-female surgery is not

a severance; post-op, a penis wouldn't lie
intact upon a silver tray. The surgery is realignment,
tissue scraped to hollow out the male member, penile

skin then tucked inside to shape a new vagina.
Vaginoplasty is creation, not removal.
It's not a loss, a cause for grief, but gain.

These surgeons aren't assailants, but gardeners
restoring the should-be-ness
of the body-in-waiting.

BO(D)Y-IN-WAITING

so powerful is the imperative to structure experience with absolute categories that figures who seemingly defy classification – such as mulattos, freaks, transvestites, bisexuals and other hybrids – elicit anxiety, hostility, or pity and are always rigorously policed

Rosemarie Garland-Thomson

Missing

Déjà vu, meltwater in the bones. 'Since my wife
died I feel like my arm's been cut off.' At home, he hears
phantom sounds, thinks she's running a bath. In the street

she reappears, phantom back, phantom hair. Pain,
displacement, an itch. Actual amputations: from
the shoulder down an emptiness but that place above

the elbow needs a scratch. What was once, now isn't,
yet still somehow is. The particular sensation
might be of use: feeling from an absent limb

lets amputees embrace prosthesis, settle to a new-
embodied self. This prologue forms a long run or roll
toward my thesis: crossing sex and phantom bodies,

cripples, legs and other parts.

The Tower Behind the Forest

When I met my love he'd been asleep for years,
his house was in a forest, Hawthorn Close. (Yet,

he'd finished a degree at forty, chatted up a woman
at a party in the weeks before we met. Things

are not always how we remember them.) I hold
in double-vision this picture of his home: elderflower tree

at gate, a smell of damp rising from the moat,
stalagmites of music mags, Calor gas heaters.

And there, on the sofa, a Sleeping Handsome prince,
who in the street walked too fast, who in the bars

played pool too well. I thought he was a woman
when we met, recall our cagey advance

and lustful attraction. Email, trains, cars.
Friday arrivals, Sunday departures.

Knowledge

I put my arm behind my head and shut my eyes – I still
know my arm is there. People feel their bodies' absences,
a proprioceptive grace. Those who are trans know their bodies
beyond looking, beyond reflections in a mirror, have

a feeling for absence as presence, whether that be
for an altered voice, smooth skin (or beard), more (or less) chest.
It is a doubling ontology. To hold both at once exerts
a pressure, puts human existence on the line – am/am not –

tautology. One can only become transsexual by denial,
by stating one is not the sex one believes in, by stating
one requires a crossing over. I am thinking about a boy
who has always been, *always* been a boy but… contra/diction.

Corridor, 1973

Nathan was aggrieved by some of his teachers and chose
to stand up to their rule. It was an all-girls school,

1973. Nate's defence of others may have been
a way of being seen. Wanting to be a classroom hero

Nate flouted rules repeatedly, was sent out from maths class.
He saw a lot of corridor; was later asked to see a shrink.

He had by then (without the aid of internet)
found a group in London. He'd written a letter to them

and received a letter back, to a Miss —. But never mind,
the letter was something. Nate then made a first request

for sex-change interventions. Explaining why
such surgery would be wrong the doctor said

It would be like cutting off the legs of a cripple.

Flood

Nathan, a walking-able youth, was told 'you are a cripple'.
Exactly what was meant by this stayed off the table.

Around the time the adult Nate told me this, he would wake
every morning and weep. Each morning there'd be

dampness on pillow, sheet and skin,
then he would get up, our day would begin.

No accompaniment to this salt-wet silence
no words, no storytelling, no dream or dreams

unfurling, no further information. Till then
I'd believed in a talking tradition that demanded

verbal attentions, catharsis, self-revelation.
I stopped myself. Shut up.

Lay beside him
and waited.

He wept and I waited.

Phantom (1): Limb Difference

The phantom limb offers a body
  that believes in its absent part,
a draft of physicality,
  an itch beneath the skin that knows.

All embryos begin the same,
  slide or push their way towards
something over which a doctor might say
  'It's a girl'
    'It's a boy'
      'It…' (ch)

Three Wishes?

It would be like cutting off the legs of a cripple.
Did he mean, a cripple might walk one day,

let's not harm his legs for now? Or did he mean,
you're sick, and this won't fix you?

Three times over decades Nate asked for relief,
asked for a better fit. Three times he was refused.

Do I shape this story as fairytale?
Yet if I ask how many doctors he tried,

there is no ready number. Nate's still
in an empty corridor missing arithmetic.

Phantom (ii): Growth

Not exactly absence then, un-
fittedness occurs. Cells convex
instead of concave, turn out
instead of in,
create a conjecture
of human be(com)ing.

This is Not a Stunt

Invert theory grew from exploring
hermaphrodites' bodies, dead and alive.
Finding a 'true sex', not a spectrum,

was the sexologists' grail,
those who couldn't live
in their findings, jailed or ostracised.

Marriages broken.
Unruly hermaphrodites
were placed in asylums alongside

those who had no trace of
biological bothness, people living
by their own self-knowledge.

Victorian asylums enforced
gendered clothing, re-education.
Guards with flaming swords stood at gates.

One soul, asylumed as a man,
wrote to Carl Westphal.
The letter self-combusted in Carl's hands.

Freud later thought that invert males
were deviants caused by
arrested development, and invert females

repressed homosexuals
or narcissists when loving women.
Not much has changed:

deviant, freak, liar, con. Though
documentaries now get screened
pre-watershed. Not evil any more,

sensational instead!
What fun for the press.
Here we are then,

stunt-men and -women without fire-suits.
Watch us stumble, lift our arms
like flaming swords.

Life Support

It would be like cutting off the legs of a cripple.

There are cases where cutting off a person's legs
might be advantageous: gangrene, for example, frostbite,

that condition where the legs grow large and heavy
like an elephant's. Post-removal the patient

might not run but they might become more agile.
Some become so heavy in their bodies they attempt

self-removal.
You'd think about it too, if every day you

were taken for someone, some/body else: a man
or woman you're not. 'Sir? … so sorry, *Miss.*'

Phantom (III): Phobia

Transgress. Trans/gression.
Aggression against transsexuals.
Let me show you those people made
angry seeing a person on the street,
unable to tell 'what' that person is,
their fury in your face – how can a soul exist?

A Self-made Man

In 1946 Dr Dillon published his findings.
Dillon embodied author/ity: a doctor and a writer
but was a man born female. He came from money,

helpful when the rest is stacked against you,
went to a women's college then had his records changed
so he could enter med school Michael.

Dillon marked off the observed sex of bodies
from the sex that was self-knowledge;
levered both away from sexual desire. A new

discussion opened (in some quarters). Westphal's
inverts were gone, Freud's repressions, gone.
Finally, a new term. A crossing.

Meltwater

We were in bed at Hawthorn Close.
Those mornings slip anchor, our mattress sets sail,

the rough trajectory, the backward thrust of memory
suggests this was ten years ago, but we might have sailed

at anytime. There are some kinds of wave that sweep every
thing – clocks and mirrors, books and conversations,

all props and underpinnings – away.
Ice thaws.

Don't think
I think I rescued my love, he rescued himself.

The season changed in the forest of glances,
water ebbed.

Flow

Back in the corridor
a thirteen-year-old boy –

caught in the conundrum
of his already-being

yet body not matching –
has periods, the wrong

kind of chest. (Shh-shhh, we do not
use those words. This is not happening.)

It would be like cutting off the legs of a cripple.

But Nate thought
  No.

It would be like offering me wheels,
giving me freedom and movement.

Corridor, 2013

These days I reflect on the absent cripple in that doctor's
simile. The cripple is taken from reality and shifted

ontologically. In the 1970s few would have baulked
at such a term. But still, to have used this other state of being,

to try and explain his refusal to act on Nathan's behalf,
was muddled. There is an analogy, but not the one he made.

It's wrong to have said this to that lad, it's wrong to have used
this line at all, suggesting disability's a lost cause,

as though its usefulness lies only in simile or metaphor.
Which brings us back to the phantom limb. Since a phantom

is usually thought of as dead, a ghost absent/present, a soul
in some distress, this won't do anymore.

A trans person's body lives, their bodily knowledge
is *warm*, is not to be found lying dead in a surgeon's tray.

It is a schoolboy in a corridor, outside a maths room,
facing a door, wearing a girls' school uniform,

not a phantom, though he knows he is not seen.
Nate chews the inside of his cheek, kicks against the wall,

inks letters on his arm, daydreams. He shouldn't be here.
He shouldn't *be*…

Nate scrapes his nail against his thumb, unpicks his skin.
Stop. No more metaphors –

that time is done.
These are my lover's limbs, waiting.

* * *

Déjà vu

Your friend said years ago that you looked like
Alain Delon. But you didn't know what he looked like,
except in his later movies. Now, we are sitting
in front of *The Leopard*, three hours long
with subtitles. Delon is in it, young.

Burt Lancaster plays the lead,
Don Fabrizio Salina. His children
are grown and his nephew (played by Alain Delon)
a sometime suitor to one of his daughters. I didn't know
Burt spoke Italian that well. I didn't know Burt

spoke Italian at all. But it's not good enough for Visconti:
Burt's dubbed over. The silenced leopard mouths
Italian, with Italian voiceover and English subs.
When revolution takes Italy, Salina's family
take a holiday. When Salina says, with a sigh,

'What it is to be' – old? middle aged? – 'forty-five,'
we are shocked. Burt seems an old man, at least
sixty-five in this film. People looked older back then,
aged faster ... I wonder what Delon
looks like these days? Then he played Tancredi

Falconeri, a bird of prey pursuing
Angelica Sedàra, a part played by Claudia
Cardinale, another bird,
modern with her chignon and
early sixties makeup. The youngsters

have sided with then against Garibaldi.
The Don sickens of politics as everything
changes, everything stays the same. Feeling ill,
he flees an all-night party leaving
a message for his wife and daughters to make

their own way home in the carriage; though sick,
he will walk. It's barely dawn. A priest
crosses his path. The Don kneels to cross himself;
struggles to stand. I'd like to see him die now,
the story demands it, but Salina lives.

He turns his back on us and walks into
an alleyway. The screen darkens. This ending
feels wrong, is incomplete. Despite a too-long
history lesson now the film's too short.
Even though little else can come

except a death, I want to know, I want to see…
Even though Salina is both silenced
and dubbed, I want to hear him speak some more.
Burt was fifty that year. You are forty-eight,
and yes, the young Delon looked a little like you

nine years ago, the time we met: all cheekbones
and eyebrows, prettily handsome. Yet now
who would see the resemblance?
I place your square head beside Burt's.
Your voice has changed too.

On Life Writing

I didn't want to write a noble story, or a poem full
of overcoming, I didn't want much story here at all.
Stories sap our social view, a politics of knowing,
invoke instead individual triumph: The Quest, An Epic Love,

The Monster Overcome. Balderdash and fireworks.
I didn't want to replicate the romance of *The Gargoyle,*
its masculinity-in-peril with attendant female angel,
nor imitate *The English Patient,* I'm no heroic nurse,

instead, I feel quite lucky in my loving, being loved.
The fact is we're ordinary. Transition is not
an ending, though it might seem that way.
Given a narrative arc, then yes, perhaps we're past

the obvious crisis, but who's to say what lies ahead?
Who's to say our story's over? There's moments, weeks
of angst when the national supply of Sustanon
runs out. Or after his annual blood check, results show

'an anomaly, please contact your doctor'.
And oh, how we laugh when this turns out to be
'slightly raised cholesterol'.
We're middle-aged, of course. Life rolls on.

The Tunnel

I'm thinking about going home, going
home to you. Even when you stay in your room,
just say 'hello' as I walk in, in fact that's what

you mostly do, the thought of you, the coming
home thought of you is powerful as
a talisman, a spell around my drowsy head.

People surge onto the train. A hum
of sweaty sausage-rolls envelops us.
I slump lower in my less-than-Virgin seat.

We expand and contract in this
dank rabbit hutch, burrow fiercely
through the dark.

Once I had a dog. Coming home, a welcome –
even when she was old, a sculling tail would
beat the floor. Habits, we should praise them more,

the slow forms of knowledge, what's held on the backs
of the eyes after the sun goes down: love confirmed
by presence, not gesture or romance or show,

a defence against the dark arts, not much
in the way of conversation, no action, no story, no plot,
but what will come after all that,

the home at the heart of the poem.
Absolute dark,
then the door and the tail and the breath.

Fathom

Between the hours of two and four
our muscles slacken, heartbeats slow,
if needs we'll slip our mortal coil
on this night tide: deep breaths, let go.

Between the hours of two and four
most people pass away if passing
in their sleep is what they'll do.
Don't be alarmed, this is the death

we'd all choose, asleep in bed.
The hours of two and three and four
are those when analgesics reign,
we slip with ease through that last door,

but other slippage has its place
between these hours, slip in, drift low.
Watch: this quietest ebb will even out
the balance sheet of loss, will pace

our bodies' sighs and dreams. Balm pours
into our bones and loosens joints, so
most births take place at night
between the hours of two and four.

Chiaroscuro

The pond made winter's bed
from blackened sycamore leaves,

now green arms razzle through the waterline.

Marsh marigolds hold out their cups
shout, Look at me! Look at me,

don't I do yellow exceptionally well?

Notes

'CLOTH EARS'

David Lodge. *Deaf Sentence.* 2009. London: Penguin

'TONI & GUY'

Flesh was a hedonistic queer clubnight at the Hacienda, hence the capital 'F'.

'THE VIOLENCE OF'

Sharon Olds. 1987. 'Outside the Operating Room of the Sex Change Doctor' in *The Gold Cell,* New York: Knopf

BO(D)Y-IN-WAITING

Rosemarie Garland Thompson. 1997. *Extraordinary Bodies: Figuring Physical Disability in American Culture and Literature.* New York: Columbia University Press, p.34.

'MISSING'

Jillian Weiss says, 'I used to count the number of phantom limbs that cropped up in poems; the phantom limb is typically a metaphor for the loss of a loved one. This has always struck me as funny because my phantom limb is ticklish rather than painful'. Ed. Bartlett, Black and Norton, 2011. In *Beauty is a Verb*: *The New Poetry of Disability*. Cinco Puntos Press: El Paso, p.143-144.

Jay Prosser. 1998. *Second Skins: The Body Narratives of Transsexuality.* New York: Columbia University Press. ppP.78-90 discusses proprioceptive feeling for transsexuals as a way of exploring self-knowledge independent of a mirror.

'CORRIDOR, 1973'

My partner and I discussed this poem sequence, and we do remember things slightly differently. We agreed on a fictional name for the teenage boy.

'PHANTOM (I): LIMB DIFFERENCE' and 'PHANTOM (II): GROWTH'

An intersex person born exhibiting unclear bodily evidence of being either a boy or a girl may be subjected to unwanted cosmetic genital surgeries that may later reduce sexual sensation and/or cause pain and urinary problems. This intervention is now banned in the UK on purely cosmetic grounds ('to look right'), in part because of campaigns by intersex adults who had been subjected to such surgeries as children. In contrast a trans person may actively want surgical interventions and then be refused them. If we accept the in-between-ness and biological complexity of the intersex person it is not a huge leap to accept the trans person's existence as another place on a spectrum of possibilities. See Catherine Harper. 2007. *Intersex.* Oxford; New York: Berg.

'THIS IS NOT A STUNT'

In the nineteenth century medical men attempted to deny sexual uncertainties in nature and society by reducing the numbers of hermaphrodites on record by divining their 'true' sex and establishing them as either male or female. Alice

Dormurat Dreger gives historical accounts of intersex people's case studies, and explores the fears of their doctors (2000, *Hermaphrodites and the Medical Invention of Sex.* Cambridge, MA; London: Harvard University Press).

For more on the sexologists Havelock-Ellis and Westphal, see Prosser, 1998, pp.135-169. Havelock-Ellis was the expert Radclyffe Hall enlisted for an endorsement of her account of an invert's life in her infamous novel, *The Well of Loneliness.*

Freud's diagnosis of 'repressed homosexual' was devised after reading Daniel Paul Schreber's published memoir. Schreber saw rays of light, divine beings and believed that God was turning him into His female consort. This is discussed in Mary Elene Wood's *Life Writing and Schizophrenia: Encounters on the Edge of Meaning* (2013, Amsterdam; New York: Rodopi). Wood does not discuss the possibility that Schreber might have been trans, but she does argue that hallucinations and hearing voices rarely occur without the dominant culture's social influence (e.g. racist or sexist ideologies often occur and impact negatively on those in the grip of hallucinations). This in no way suggests I think trans people are delusional, simply that some people with delusions/voices/visions might ALSO be trans. Past medical practice and the dominant culture has overlooked this.

'LIFE SUPPORT'

In 2011 the NHS gave figures of 140,000 suicide attempts in an adult population of around 50,893,000. This suggests a 1 in 3,000 chance of attempted suicide amongst the general population. LGBT surveys and health reports have stated that LGBs come close to 1 in 6 attempting suicide, with trans people more likely at 1 in 2 or 1 in 3 (Prosser, 1998).

'PHANTOM (III): PHOBIA'

Remembering Our Dead is a website dedicated to documenting violence against transsexuals. [www.gender.org/remember]

'A SELF-MADE MAN'

Michael Dillon, 1946. *Self: A Study in Ethics and Endocrinology.* London: Heinemann

'ON LIFE WRITING'

Trans people don't just take hormones to transition but must continue to take them for the rest of their lives. Sustanon is a form of testosterone given to trans men that can be injected fortnightly at home. There was a nationwide shortage in 2011. The replacement was more viscous and, as it required a bigger bore needle, had to be injected by a nurse once every three months.

AFTERWORD

Wallace Stevens. 1954. 'Man Carrying Thing' in *The Collected Poems of Wallace Stevens.* New York: Knopf.

John Keats, Letter to George and Thomas Keats, Sunday 21 December 1817. 2009. *John Keats Selected Letters.* Oxford: Oxford University Press.

Robert Frost. 1964. *Robert Frost Selected Letters.* University of California: Holt, Rinehart and Winston.

Afterword

In putting together this collection I have sometimes doubted whether the poems were sufficiently poem-y. After all, 'the poem must resist the intelligence / Almost entirely successfully' (Wallace Stevens). It may be that a few of my poems pull too far towards a fixed meaning. Robert Frost described a poem as being a balance between 'the sense of sound' and 'the sound of sense'. Possibly my poems are too much concerned with their sense, too prosaic. The difficulty for me is that I wished to explore what it is to be male or female and intersex or transsexual, and once there, maintaining clear pronoun use *and* poetic diction became tricky.

Some of the time, like Keats, we can exist in negative capability, that is, we can exist in 'uncertainties, Mysteries, doubts, without any irritable reaching after fact and reason.' We don't need an explanation; we can just be. But some of the time I think we do want clarity. A poem may be slippery, and I'm fine with that, but if it becomes too unmoored from meaning then I defeat my own purposes. When a body is shaped too far from a person's gender identity they too may come unmoored. Out task is to find our balance points.

I take heart from a person who heard some of the *Bo(d)y-in-waiting* poems during their development. She said she understood that feeling of living within a perceived doubleness and being judged. She was mixed race and sometimes both black people and white people would say to her, 'but isn't that confusing for you?' She was not confused, she knew what she was and how she felt: it was other people who didn't get it. This woman's ability to project herself into the poems, despite them not being about her, was deeply reassuring.

I hope that you, the reader, also find space in the poems.

CSN 2016

69